The Princess
&
The Sea-Bear

POLESTAR
BOOK PUBLISHERS

Published by
Polestar Press Ltd., R.R. 1, Winlaw, B.C., V0G 2J0, 604-226-7670

Distributed by
Raincoast Book Distribution Ltd., 112 East 3rd Avenue,
Vancouver, B.C., V5T 1C8, 604-873-6581

Canadian Cataloguing in Publication Data
Skogan, Joan, 1945-
The princess and the sea-bear and other
Tsimshian stories
Originally published: Prince Rupert, B.C.:
Metlakatla Band Council, 1983.
ISBN 0-919591-54-X
1. Tsimshian Indians - Legends - Juvenile
literature. 2. Indians of North America -
British Columbia - Legends - Juvenile
literature. I. Stewart, Claudia. II. Title.
E99.T8S56 1990   J398.2'089974   C90-091153-0

Acknowledgements
Published with the assistance of the Canada Council
Illustrated by Claudia Stewart
Designed by Jim Brennan
Produced by Polestar Press in Winlaw, B.C.
Printed in Canada
Special thanks to the Museum of Northern British Columbia
"Fog Woman's Gift" originally appeared in
The Canadian Children's Anthology
"The Princess & The Sea-Bear" was produced on The Hornby
Collection, CBC Radio, Vancouver, under the title
"The Nighttime Husband."

Introduction

THE TSIMSHIAN LEGENDS are a special legacy for the modern world. They form an intricate pattern that includes earth, sea, and sky with all living creatures. In the legends, humans were united with natural and supernatural forces. Sometimes the myths continued to evolve, becoming folk tales which may feature remembered family or clan history. Through the stories the Tsimshian told one another to explain their world, we can glimpse the wholeness of their lives.

This land has been changed by the twentieth century, but we can still recognize the settings of the tales. They are close to us in time. At the beginning of this century, anthropologists recorded many of the legends from those who heard them as children when the coast was home only to its first people.

The myths reflect the coastal environment physically, and as it was perceived by its peoples. Here are the long sea journeys, the rocky shores and sheltered bays, the secrets of mountains and rivers. The legends are rich in characters: bear, deer, wolf, salmon, and all the creatures who share the land and sea with man. The action is strong, sometimes heroic, sometimes foolish, and the connection between events is often subtle or assumed, with motives too ambiguous for us to fully understand. The theme of the legends is always clear: the cycle of spiritual and earthly dependance that links humanity with all forms of life.

This circle of connected life is lost to us. The sea and the mountains and the salmon are here, but most of us cannot know a reality in which man is only part of the mystery. Once, the deer was killed, the bark taken from the cedar tree, and the argillite from the mountains only in balance with human need and responsibility. The legends reveal that earlier reality. They are meant to be spoken, murmured to children picking berries on a sunny hillside, or recited around the fire on a winter night.

The Princess
and the Sea-Bear

LONG AGO a Tsimshian Indian princess sat alone on the beach in front of the village in Metlakatla Pass. Behind her were cedar longhouses and the children of the village laughing and running about the cooking fires. Before her were the changing waters of the northern sea. The princess's house was set apart from the others because she was considered special by all of her people. Even so, she was lonely, for the time had come for her to marry and have children of her own, but there seemed to be no man right for her.

Young noblemen came from villages as far away as Alaska to ask if she would marry them, but the princess was wise as well as beautiful. She listened to her grandmother who said, "Feel their hands! A smooth-handed man is soft and weak and will never make a good husband for you." So when the young men came to her, stepping proudly from their canoes loaded with gifts of sea otter pelts and abalone shells, the princess felt their hands. All of the young men were too wellborn to work. Even their canoes were paddled by other men. Their hands were smooth and the princess would have none of them. So she sat on the beach alone and looked at the sea.

That night, the princess covered herself with her fur robe and fell asleep to dream of a husband whose face she could not see. Perhaps she thought she was still dreaming when someone lay down beside her. She felt his hands and they were warm and rough so she knew this man was meant to be her husband. All night he stayed with her, but in the hour before dawn he left saying, "You must never see my face or I shall not be able to come to you again." When the sun was up, the princess came out of her little house and saw an enormous halibut lying on the beach in front of her door. She smiled to see the present from her new husband and ran to tell her grandmother about the man who had come to her in the night.

Soon all the Tsimshians knew. Their curiosity was great and the princess told them of her husband's warning never to look on his face. She shared the halibut with everyone in the village and that night her husband came again and left before morning light. This time, she found a pile of spring salmon in front of her door.

Every night he came. Every morning there was a gift from the sea for the princess. She and her grandmother traded the fish for many things and they both became wealthy. The princess was happy, but her grandmother never ceased to wonder about the nighttime husband. She gave her granddaughter a small stone pot filled with red ochre and persuaded the princess to mark him with it so they might know him in the daytime. The princess put a dab of red paint on the back of her husband's head and next day her grandmother looked carefully at all the young men in the village, but none was marked with paint. Messengers traveled to other villages further north and along the great rivers, but they found no man with the red sign.

At last the grandmother could live with her curiosity no longer. She crept from the longhouse when the stars were still shining on Metlakatla Pass and hid herself behind a tree near the beach.

As always, the princess's husband left her asleep in her furs and stepped out of the little house, but the grandmother could not see him clearly in the dark. The thin light of dawn opened the sky and she heard a splash as the nighttime husband entered the water. The next night she again looked out from her hiding place. This time she saw him.

The nighttime husband was the sea-bear — the grizzly with a fin on his back. He was towing a whale for the princess's morning gift. The great bear saw the grandmother watching him. He roared with anger and sorrow, loud enough to shake the tall cedars. For the last time, he stood on the beach, and the waking villagers listened, trembling, to his roaring song of farewell to the princess. He returned to the sea, and his body became rock which the Tsimshians ever after called Bear Rock. The princess wept for the loss of her sea-bear husband, and though the world has changed since that time, Bear Rock is still here and close by is the village of Metlakatla.

Gamlugyides and the Prince of the Wolves

LONG AGO, in the time when there were many villages on the north coast, the Tsimshian chief Gamlugyides lived with his people beside Metlakatla Pass. The Metlakatla people lived well until the winter of the great storms and hunger. The time for oolichans and salmon to return to the rivers and berries to ripen in the summer sun was still far off. Wind whipped the seas and snow covered the land. Even the strongest man could not fish or hunt. The people ate the dried fish they had left and huddled close to one another around the fires in the longhouses.

The chief Gamlugyides woke early one morning and lay on his sleeping platform, listening. He heard the children whimpering in their sleep. He heard the small sounds of his weary people preparing for another day, and from the hills above the village, he heard the howling of wolves. Their cries rose high and mournful, one howl overriding the rest. Everyone in the village heard the wolves, and they feared them as a sign of further trouble.

The next morning Gamlugyides woke early again and listened to the wolves. He walked through the village to where the cedar and spruce trees grew thick at the bottom of the hill, and stood there alone. Around him the howling rose and fell in the early morning mist. He imagined he heard his name in the cry that was louder and higher than the rest. "Come, Gamlugyides," the wolves seemed to say. Four times the wolves called early in the morning. Four times Gamlugyides listened, thinking he heard his name. On the fourth morning, he heard again the call, "Come, Gamlugyides! Come and help me." He returned to the longhouse and gathered his nephews around him. "Prepare to come with me into the woods. I am going to meet the wolves."

The men disappeared into the dark forest. The howling continued while the people of the village waited and feared. The wolf pack with their chief in the centre surrounded the men. The Prince of the Wolves, pitifully weak and thin, lay whimpering in the snow as the Metlakatla chief approached. "What do you want of me?" said Gamlugyides. The great wolf opened his mouth and Gamlugyides saw a deer bone lodged sideways in his throat. "Lie still, brother, and I will help you," said the chief. He reached into the wolf's mouth to pull out the bone while the Prince of the Wolves lay at his feet and licked his hand. Gamlugyides said, "Go, brother, and do not forget me," and he and his nephews returned to the village.

Early the following morning, the wolves howled and Gamlugyides once more heard his name in their cries. He and his nephews went into the woods without fear, and the wolves leaped and danced around them. When the wolf-pack ran off, the chief saw that they had left four freshly-killed deer on the ground.

The people of Metlakatla filled their empty bellies with meat. All that long winter the wolves killed deer and other animals and left them on the hill. Gamlugyides gave food away to other villages, then traded for all that he and his people needed and became a wealthy man. He and his family had a great pole made to stand before their longhouse, a pole with the Prince of the Wolves and the chief Gamlugyides carved together as brothers.

Gamlugyides
and the Weeping Woman

THE MEETING between Gamlugyides and the Prince of the Wolves in the winter of starvation became a tale to be told around the fire, and the people of Metlakatla were content once more. Their longhouses were stacked with baskets of dried salmon and halibut and cedar boxes of oolichan grease from the Nass River. Their hunting brought much meat to the village. The joy of the hunt then, not the need for meat, caused Gamlugyides to prepare to hunt alone one fall morning. He took with him his spear, his bone knife, and a small pot of the ointment made from the devil's club plant in case he should need to strengthen himself with its power.

Gamlugyides climbed the hill overlooking Metlakatla Pass, and the sounds of the sea and the village were soon behind him. Swiftly, he made his way along the trails the deer had threaded through a summer's growth of salal and ferns. The sun lit the tops of the cedars high above him. The early morning chill faded from the air. Winter was coming, but this bright day was before him and Gamlugyides was glad to be hunting alone.

Suddenly he stopped, startled by the sound of wild sobbing coming from the thickly wooded slope above him. He stood

thoughtful for a moment, then he smiled. Once again, the Metla-katla chief was going to encounter a supernatural being. Many times he had heard stories of Crying Woman, the magically powerful spirit-woman whose false tears and mournful child frightened anyone who tries to take her powers for himself. Carefully, Gamlugyides smeared the devil's club ointment on his arms and shoulders and set out to follow Crying Woman.

After a time he saw her — a dark, hooded figure with a bundle on her back. She ran crying out to Gamlugyides, "Go away. Do not come near." But the chief closed his ears to her sorrowful warnings and ran after her. He reached for the child and Crying Woman whirled around to scratch his arms with her copper claws. The devil's club ointment strengthened Gamlugyides. He grasped the child firmly and ran on. Crying Woman shrieked with rage and clawed him again and again.

All day they ran. The salmonberry brambles whipped their faces and the salal tangled their footsteps while the wailing of the Crying Woman shattered the silence of the forest. Late in the day Gamlugyides called, "If you will give me your powers, I will return your child."

Crying Woman answered, "Give me the child and I will reward you with these gifts." As she spoke, a pile of furs appeared before Gamlugyides. The glossy pelts of wolverine, otter, and mink tempted the chief greatly. He looked at his arms where blood from the wounds Crying Woman had dealt him mingled with streaks of the devil's club ointment.

"No," he said.

"I will give you more." And the pile of furs grew until it stood as high as Gamlugyides himself. He almost weakened. The furs would bring him incredible wealth. He straightened his shoulders, shook his head, and gripped the child tightly. Crying Woman screamed and tore at him, but he neither moved nor spoke. At last she exhausted her anger.

Gamlugyides said, "Give me your powers, then I will return your child."

"Let it be so," sighed the spirit-woman. Her tears ceased. She drew from her hood a shirt of finely woven cedar bark. "Put on this shirt and never take it off, or you will lose the powers I give you. Others will be jealous of you. Never tell them of the shirt and how you came by it, or they will destroy you." Gamlugyides put on the shirt and felt a surge of confidence and strength. He gave the child to Crying Woman and she returned to the forest, leaving no sign.

Gamlugyides passed his hands over the furs she had left behind. They were so many he would have to order his nephews to pack them down to his longhouse. He smoothed the magical shirt, unseen now under his cloak, and set out along the trail back to Metlakatla.

Gamlugyides and the Faithless Wife

THE MAGIC SHIRT that Gamlugyides won from Crying Woman brought luck to the Metlakatla chief and his people. Everything Gamlugyides did was successful. When he hunted in the forest, he returned with many deer, and when he traveled over the ocean hunting for seal, his heavily laden canoe always returned safely. Chiefs from other villages journeyed to Metlakatla to trade or buy food from him. Gamlugyides' wealth became great. Besides these riches, Gamlugyides now had the gift of healing, and he had cured many of his people of sickness.

All knew that the chief had received his great powers from a supernatural source, but he never spoke of it. As Crying Woman had predicted, some were jealous of the power. Among these jealous ones was another chief, the brother of Gamlugyides' youngest, most beautiful wife. This man plotted with his sister, saying to her, "Your husband is too powerful. You must find the secret of his power so we may destroy it for the safety of our own family." At this time, the Nishga woman who was also wife to Gamlugyides warned him of those who feared him and would try to trick away his power. But Gamlugyides had grown very sure of himself. He laughed at her and paid no heed to her warning.

Gamlugyides' youngest wife began to charm him. She cooked him special delicacies and attended willingly to his every wish. One night as they lay together in their sleeping place, she said in her low, sweet voice, "Husband, how do you keep your powers? Tell me, please."

Gamlugyides replied, "I have a symbol of my power, but it is hidden in the mountains so none may find it." He slept peacefully that night. The young woman crept to the shadows behind the longhouse where her brother waited.

"You will never overcome Gamlugyides," she told him. "His power is hidden in the hills."

This lesser chief took the news to the wise men of his own family who thought on it for some time before they announced, "Impossible! Gamlugyides' power is such that he has his magic close to him at all times. She must persuade him to tell where it lies."

So the youngest wife made herself even more pleasing to Gamlugyides. She tended to him in all ways, and he was well satisfied with her. When they were lying together, she said, "Why did you tell me your power is hidden in the mountains? I have seen that you do not go into the hills before you hunt the seal. Please tell me. I wish only to help guard your strength." Gamlugyides did not reply. As he slept, his young wife lay beside him, planning to ask him again the following night.

She waited until Gamlugyides was almost asleep, then softly she asked him where lay his powers. A sleepy Gamlugyides murmured, "I get my gift from my shirt. I will never take it off, for if I did, all my powers would vanish." His wife knew he spoke the truth. Never did Gamlugyides remove his finely woven cedar bark shirt. When she told her brother she had discovered the truth at last, he gave her a shell knife and ordered

her to cut off the shirt as Gamlugyides slept.

The next day Gamlugyides paddled far out to sea to guide the young hunters on their first trip to the seal grounds. He slept heavily that night, feeling nothing when his faithless wife cut the shirt from his body. At dawn he woke, strangely weak. He put out his hand to touch his cedar shirt. It was gone. Gamlugyides had lost his special powers. After a time he summoned his strength and woke his Nishga wife.

Gamlugyides' pride would not allow him to remain in Metla-katla, so he and the Nishga woman gathered together their family and prepared to leave. Gamlugyides and the others journeyed to the Nass River, home of the Nishga people, where they formed the household of Towq, the wolf. But the story of Gamlugyides and the shirt he received from Crying Woman were long re-membered in Metlakatla, his first home.

Strong Man
Who Holds Up the World

AGES AGO, when many of the Tsimshian people lived in Metla-katla Passage, the chief of one of the villages had four sons. The three older boys were lively, but the youngest one seemed lazy and slow, and the others often teased him.

The time came for the men of the village to prepare for the sea lion hunt. Far across the northern seas lay the rocky island where the sea lions gathered. The waves roared and crashed over the island. A man had to be able to leap to the rocks and overcome the huge beasts, or be killed himself.

The three older brothers were training for the hunt. Every morning they swam in the ocean to accustom their bodies to the cold. When they returned, their father, the chief, lashed their backs with berry branches to harden the boys to pain. They drank a brew from the devil's club plant, and wrenched the branches from spruce trees to develop their strength. While they tested themselves, their younger brother lay in the warm ashes beside the fire. His brothers scorned and insulted him saying, "We would starve if we depended on you to hunt for us." But the boy slept on by the fire.

Unknown to the others, while they slept at night, the youngest

boy swam alone in the cold, dark waters of the Pass. His body slipped easily through the waves as he swam out further than the others had ever been, and each night went a little further yet. He lashed his own back with branches, and sipped the devil's club tea before he slept by the fire. His brothers teased, "You are covered with ashes. Don't you ever bathe?" But he said nothing to them.

One night when he was swimming, a loon came towards him as if to speak. "What do you have to tell me, supernatural one?" said the boy.

The loon answered, "I have strength to give you, Brother. Take hold of my feet and we will dive together." The boy held onto the loon, and they dove to the bottom of the sea where a cave appeared. The loon instructed the boy, "Enter the cave and bathe in the spring you will find there. When you return to your village, you too must practice breaking the branches of the spruce trees. Say nothing of this to anyone."

The youngest brother did these things, and his strength grew until he could bend the spruce tree to the ground. All in the village were bitter against him now, yet he said nothing of his secret practices.

On the morning of the sea lion hunt, the older brothers took their harpoons with cedar lines, and stepped into the canoes. The youngest brother rose from his place by the fire, and walked to the beach. "I will go with you," he said, but his uncles and the older men angrily refused to take him, saying, "You should have prepared yourself. A lazy, dirty fool like you will only be in the way."

His youngest uncle took pity on him. "You can come with me — surely you can help in some small ways. Perhaps you will learn something." The hunters paddled their canoes, lifting and falling on the long swells, until they heard the roaring of the sea lions on the high, barren rock.

One of the uncles stood in the bow of the first canoe and made ready to leap as it climbed the wave crest, but another wave caught them and crushed the canoe on the rocks. The men fell into the sea and were lost. The other hunters hung back. Then the youngest brother stood, balancing himself in the rolling canoe, calling "I shall jump to the rock." Though the others believed he, too, would drown, they could not stop him. He leaped and clung to the rock, then ran to attack the largest sea lion. He thrust the animal over and broke its back. He killed several more sea lions before the rest escaped, then he slung the carcasses into the canoes plunging in the wild seas around the island. Every house in the village was rich with meat. For a time there was no more talk about the laziest boy in Metlakatla.

The youngest brother was growing to manhood, but he continued in his sleepy ways. People forgot that he had proved himself strong and brave. Winter turned to spring, and the men of Metlakatla began to prepare for the competitions of strength between the northern villages. The young man still slept in the ashes. Everyone said to him, "You are filthy — why can't you be like the others?" Only his youngest uncle said, "Leave him alone. Do not forget he shamed you all once."

As before, the youngest brother swam alone at night, often meeting the loon, who advised him to practice up-rooting spruce trees to strengthen himself. This the young man did, until he could tear the largest trees from the earth and cast them into the ocean.

Those from distant villages gathered together with the people of Metlakatla for the tribal contests. A large pile of stones was collected for the first contest. For days the men took turns throwing. A man from the Nass River threw farther than the others, and his people were excited and taunted the Metlakatla people. When the young man who slept by the fire offered to take part, his own people yelled, "Filthy One, you have not trained at all! Do not bring any more shame upon us!" But the youngest brother smiled, saying "These stones you have used are fit only for children." He chose a huge boulder from the beach, and threw it past the stone of the Nass River man. His people danced and cheered, but the young man only wandered back to his fire.

He joined the contests again for the wrestling matches. A huge man, almost a giant, from Kitamaat Village, defeated the other competitors. The Kitamaat people laughed and jeered, "Where is the Filthy One? He was lucky before. Let us see what he can do." When he whom they called "Filthy One" came to meet the Kitamaat champion, he seemed in danger of being killed by the giant. The Kitamaat man rushed forward, but the youngest brother grasped him and threw his body into the air, overcoming him completely. All the people murmured among themselves, for they realized now that this young man was no ordinary person.

The final contest was the up-rooting of trees, the test of complete strength. Many men tried, but only one succeeded in pulling out a fair sized tree. The young man smiled and said, "We should not play with saplings." He wrenched from the ground the biggest spruce tree on the hill and threw it over the cliff. The people from all the villages stood in silence. This man was a supernatural being.

The young man's strength became known in all parts of the North, even the animals heard of him. One by one they came to test themselves against his strength: the cougar, the wolf, even Medeek, the great grizzly bear. The man from Metlakatla conquered them all.

The forest itself tested him. The trees crowded onto the beach, but he up-rooted them and thrust them back. He pushed away the mountains when they tried to smother the village. He was the strongest man in the world, though he still slept by the fire much of the time.

One night, when all in the village slept, a strange canoe landed on the beach in front of Metlakatla. The men in the canoe said to one another, "This is the place. This is where he lives." The steersman jumped ashore and went directly to where the strong man was sleeping.

Gently, he shook him awake. "Come, my dear, your grandfather has need of you. You are ready for your great task." Without a word, the young man followed the stranger to the canoe. The steersman said, "Let us be on our way," and the canoe became a blackfish, skimming the waves with the travelers on his back.

Far from land, they sighted a rock. Here the blackfish stopped, and they stepped from the canoe. The strangers took the form of loons, and the one who had been steersman said, "We have brought you here because your grandfather, He-Who-Holds-Up-the-World, has grown weary. He has waited for your training to be completed. Now you are ready. Come." He took the young man along a path leading into the rock. Loons and ducks guarded the trail. The man from Metlakatla entered an opening in the ground and descended a long ladder.

When he reached the bottom of the ladder, he saw a very old man with a huge hemlock pole braced against his shoulder. The aged one said, "I have waited long for you, but I had to be certain you would have the strength to do this work. Now, I will instruct you. The ducks and loons will be your messengers. They will bring your food. The blue bill duck will oil your joints, so you will never become stiff. Remember, you must stay still. If you move at all, you will cause an earthquake. Should you collapse, the world will be destroyed. Now I am going to rest." Slowly, the old one rose, and the young man took his place.

Next morning, when the people of the village did not see their strong young man beside his fire, they searched for him and were

greatly concerned. The youngest uncle said, "Surely he has been called away to some task fit for his great strength." The Tsimshian never saw the young man again, yet the earth of Metlakatla was steady beneath their feet, and today the ducks still dive deep into the sea.

Scannah
and the Beautiful Woman

LONG AGO, at the head of a bay near the present village of Metla-katla, the Tsimshian people's finest hunter walked on the beach with his wife. This woman had beauty as well as a shining spirit, and her husband loved her well. The two of them stood arm in arm in the sun, looking at the bright ocean, when they saw the body of a white sea otter drifting in on the tide.

Calling out in delight at such a rare find, the woman ran to the water's edge and waded into the waves. As the hunter watched, she and the white otter disappeared beneath the sea. Her husband swam far out looking for her and waited on the shore until near dark before he admitted to himself that she was truly gone. He returned to the village, hoping to find the truth about his great loss from Ska-geh, the One-Who-Sees-Visions.

Ska-geh crouched, silent, in a shadowed corner of the long-house as the hunter told his tale. He looked long into the fire, and after a long time he said, "The woman was taken by Scannah, the sea otter people. She is far away in their underwater home, wife to their chief. No human can rescue her."

"I shall not rest until I have tried," the hunter declared. "You must help me."

So Ska-geh instructed the sorrowing husband, "You must take two companions, the martin and the swallow, to help you on your journey. You will search the seas until you find two heads of kelp tied together. These mark the road under the ocean to the home of the Scannah people. I cannot tell what will happen to you there, but I can give you a small power that may strengthen you." The old man fastened a deerskin bag around the hunter's neck saying, "The dried leaves within will make whole that which is broken." The hunter bid farewell to all in the longhouse. Ska-geh returned to his fire.

Softly and clearly the hunter called, "Brothers, I am ready," and the martin and the swallow flew to his side. The canoe moved quickly through Metlakatla Pass to the open sea with the martin flying ahead and the swallow above. Many days the three of them traveled, seeing nothing but wind-tossed foam and sea birds, until they were near despair. At last, the martin returned to the canoe saying, "Far ahead yet, I see two kelp bulbs tied together." The three travelers went towards this place.

The hunter tied the canoe to one of the kelp heads, and he and the two birds talked together. "All we can do," said the martin, "is to separate. I will guard the canoe while you continue your journey to the home of the Scannah. The swallow shall fly home and tell our people what has happened." To this, they all agreed, and they parted in sadness with small hope of seeing each other again. The brave hunter put his hands on the kelp heads and took his first step onto the undersea road.

The way before him led to the green gloom of the undersea world. The sunlight was far above the hunter now. He knew not when he would reach the end of the road, or what he might find there.

In the world above, day had turned into night, but the hunter walked on, traveling forever downwards until he heard fearful noises ahead. A flock of geese jostled one another and muttered angrily. Their searching beaks terrified him, and he waited until he could pass among them unnoticed.

The hunter ran. He could only continue his journey now, or be lost forever in this shadowed world. Once again he stopped, his own breathing loud in his ears, when he heard sounds further along the path. Three men he thought to be slaves were taking turns chopping at an old hemlock tree. Their stone axe was clumsy and dull, and the work went slowly. As he watched, the head flew off the axe, and the slaves tried in vain to mend it. They moaned, "How shall we finish this work? The master will be angry and his rage is fierce."

From the deerskin bag Ska-geh had hung around his neck, the hunter took some of the dried leaves. He stepped forward to sprinkle the leaves over the axe, and the head came together with the handle as strong as before. The slaves stared at him in awe. When they saw that he was human, the first slave said, "How do you come to be in this world?"

"I have come from the land above to find my wife. The Scannah took her from our home to be wife for their chief."

The slaves looked at one another. The first slave spoke again, "The sea otter chief is our master, and though we fear him greatly, we will help you as you have helped us. First, you must beware of the geese. They, too, were once the Scannah chief's wives, until he tired of them. He has changed them into blind creatures to act as his messengers. Now, here is the plan."

The hunter drew close to the slaves and listened.

"The woman who was your wife in the world above will be standing beside the cooking fire," said the slave. "We will fetch water for her and spill it onto the fire." The hunter agreed that the resulting confusion would give him his only chance to rescue his wife. He and the slaves set out for the Scannah chief's dwelling place.

Soon enough they came to the fire. The hunter saw the figure

of a woman standing nearby. Her cloak was wrapped about her body as if to shield herself, and her face was hidden, but he knew this was his wife. Saying nothing, he withdrew into the shadows while the slaves took up a large cedar box and filled it with water. Even the cooking boxes here were beautifully carved with the sea otter crest. The slaves brought the box to the coals. The hunter moved a little closer to the silent woman. Suddenly, the carved box tipped and clouds of smoke and steam rose around the woman. The hunter leaped forward and clasped her in his arms. "Come, my wife!" he cried. The two of them ran, hand in hand, as the Scannah roused themselves to give chase.

They fled along the undersea road, past the quarrelsome geese, ever upwards, closer and closer to the top. The sounds of pursuit faded behind them until at last they placed their hands together on the two heads of kelp that marked the beginning of the sea road.

Their canoe was safe, still tied to the kelp, but the faithful martin lay in the bottom of the boat, faint and near death from thirst. "Oh, my brother," murmured the hunter. Gently he placed some of Ska-geh's dried leaves on the martin's body. The bird stirred to life. The hunter and his beautiful wife wept a little in thankfulness that they all lived in the sunlight once more.

They traveled home to find the swallow safe with Ska-geh, and told their adventures to all the people of the longhouse. The hunter and his wife passed the rest of their days in peace and comfort at Metlakatla.

Foam Woman
and the Sea Otter Hunters

THE TSIMSHIAN living in one of the smaller villages at Metlakatla were great sea otter hunters. They traveled often to the kelp patches where the otters gathered near Aristobel Island. The hunters were brave and skillful, but too often their canoes were caught in the rapids that surged offshore, and the men did not return.

But they had to hunt. The glossy furs were needed for their warmth, and their beauty brought needed trade goods to the village. Early one morning, almost all of the young hunters, led by their uncles and fathers wise in the ways of the sea, left for Aristobel Island. They were near the place of danger when they saw a child floating on the sea. None of the men spoke, though all trembled with the fear and glory of the sight. This child was a false vision — not a baby to be rescued, but a sign of the power of Foam Woman, the devouring monster of the whirlpool. If her child were captured, she would lose her powers.

The steersman leaned far out over the rushing water, and the others paddled desperately to keep the canoe from the sucking roar of the whirlpool. He almost grasped the child. The wind stirred into a gale and foam flew about them. The canoe tilted into the whirlpool and was seen no more. The hunters were lost.

At home, the people of the village wept. Their chief came before them in sorrow, and spoke to them. "We must hunt the sea otter to live," he said. "Foam Woman has devoured our hunters. Before we are lost as a people, we must destroy her."

Only three young men remained in the village. Together with their chief, they chose a spruce tree for a canoe. Many days the four of them laboured to make a canoe that could withstand the heaviest seas and defeat the whirlpool. They hollowed the spruce log with their stone adzes, and filled the hollow with water and hot rocks to steam and shape the curves. They carved the sea otter crest into the side with their bone and shell knives.

At last, the canoe was ready. The chief and the three young men carried it to the beach and launched it into a heavy sea. They paddled out of the bay to open water until the spruce canoe cracked with the pounding of the waves. They fought their way back and wearily pulled up the damaged canoe.

Again, the four went into the woods. This time, they chose a red cedar to make the second canoe. But even the mighty cedar cracked in the tossing seas, and the third canoe, of yellow cedar, also failed the test of strength. The year turned to winter. Storms were constant when the four men finished the last canoe made from a huge yew tree. This canoe rode the waves lightly as a leaf. The men set out to attack Foam Woman of the whirlpool.

Like their lost companions, they came close to the fierce currents and they, too, saw the false child, who is a sign of Foam Woman's powers. The child's hair floated like seaweed on the water, and the chief reached out and grasped it tightly. He held onto Foam Woman's child, shouting to the young men to make for a small island nearby.

"Give me my child," moaned Foam Woman and the winds rose. Foam whipped the air, but the chief and his men were safe on the tiny island, and they had the child. They pulled the canoe

onto the beach and climbed to the highest part of the island. In the centre of the storm they stood and watched Foam Woman whirling the waters around them, crying unceasingly for her child. "Give me my child or I will overturn the island," she threatened.

But the chief said to the others, "If the island moves, we will all get into the canoe." This they did, and the faithful yew wood craft rode the waves until the island rolled and bare rock showed. They returned to the rock and watched about them until the morning light.

Foam Woman's child died at dawn, for it had passed the night away from her. The monster woman lost her powers and the sea calmed. The chief returned the child to the sea. When it disappeared beneath the foam, he knew the whirlpool would devour no more of his people.

The four adventurers were greeted with much joy in their village, yet still all sorrowed for the ones they had lost. They turned their faces to the village opposite theirs in Metlakatla Passage. Many Tsimshian people lived in this village, and the newcomers married with them. Children were born to hunt the sea otter again at the places we know as Goose Island and Gosling Rocks, down the other side of Aristobel Island.

Rheespunt
and the Grizzly Bears

RHEESPUNT LIVED in a Tsimshian village on the Skeena River. She was a daughter of the chief, and proud of her high position. One day, this young woman set out with the other women and girls on a berry picking expedition. They had not gone far along the trail when Rheespunt stepped into a pile of bear droppings. She shrieked and stamped her feet and cursed the bears. All the long, sunny afternoon, the other women filled their baskets with red and blue huckleberries, but Rheespunt sulked and muttered about the bears. Few huckleberries went into her basket.

She lagged behind the others on the way home. When a young man appeared and said, "Let me help you with your berry basket," Rheespunt allowed him to accompany her. She did not notice when he led her along a different trail, but she was frightened when they came to a strange, dark village. A loud voice rumbled, "Bring the woman Rheespunt to me." The young man led Rheespunt before this chief and his people. Their faces and bodies were covered with bearskin robes. Rheespunt had been captured by the Bear people who were fiercely angered by her thoughtless words about them.

A new life began for proud Rheespunt. She was now a slave to

the Bears, and her days were spent gathering wood and tending the fires. The winter passed slowly. Rheespunt was often weary and sad, but spring brought new heart to her. She determined to escape. Each day she gathered wood a little further from the village, always faithfully returning to the fire, until her captors no longer watched her so closely. When Rheespunt wandered further than ever before one day, she flung down her bundle of wood and ran towards the river.

Her feet flew over the trail, but soon she heard the Bear people panting after her. She took off one of her copper bracelets to fling it behind her, and a mountain sprang up between her and the pursuing bears. Still they continued the chase. Rheespunt reached the place where the Ecstall River pours into the great Skeena and the Bears were close behind her.

She ran again. Near the island called Large Labret, now known as Balmoral, she saw a man on the river in a copper canoe. "Rescue me," she cried, "and my father will give you many gifts!" The copper canoe did not move, and the breath of the Bears was close, In desperation Rheespunt called again, "Rescue me and I will marry you." The copper canoe leapt towards her. The canoe man lifted Rheespunt into his boat, and she traveled safely down the Skeena with him. For a time, she and the copper canoe man lived alone in the slough at the mouth of the Skeena, for Rheespunt still had much to learn about living in peace with the world around her. Later, they made their home with the people of Metlakatla.

Fog Woman's Gift

IN THE TIME when animals and people were still close to one another, Raven was the hero of the northwest coast, where the mountains run down to the edge of the sea. Raven lit the dark world by tricking the chief, who lived at the head of the Nass River, into giving him the precious carved box in which the chief hid the daylight. This is the story of how Raven himself was fooled, yet once again found something of great value for the people of the coast.

Raven and his slave made camp at the mouth of a fast flowing creek. When their fire was bright and the cedar boughs were piled high for their beds, Raven said, "Tomorrow we fish for winter food."

At first light the slave paddled his master's canoe into the bay while Raven sat in the bow, baiting his lines with mussel and abalone. Raven fished for cod, he fished for sole, and he fished for halibut. All he caught were bullheads. The slave remained silent while Raven grumbled at his bad luck. "Return to camp!" he ordered, and the slave took up his paddle.

The canoe had drifted as Raven fished. Now fog smothered the sea and the far away shore. They were lost. A strand of black hair brushed Raven's face. He whirled around and beside him in the canoe was a woman whose long hair floated about her shoulders and seemed to dissolve into the mist. The slave stared at her and even Raven was too startled to speak.

Smiling, she said to him, "Give me your hat." The woman held Raven's woven cedar bark hat over the side of the canoe and the fog streamed into it, and the sun shone again.

Raven realized that the dark-haired woman was Fog Woman. Raven and his slave saw their way home clearly. When they reached the camp by the creek, Raven knew he wanted Fog Woman to be his wife. She consented to be his bride, and they were married soon afterwards.

As they made preparations for winter together, Raven planned another fishing trip. This time he went alone, leaving Fog Woman at the camp with his slave. Raven was gone so long that Fog Woman at last said to the slave, "I am hungry. Fill the water basket at the creek and bring it to me."

The slave did as she asked and set the basket before her. She dipped her finger into the water and commanded him to pour it back into the sea. As the water poured out, a bright sockeye salmon leaped from the basket. Fog Woman gave the slave a wooden club to kill the fish, and she cleaned it and propped it on green sticks by the fire. The two of them devoured the entire fish.

When their hunger was satisfied, Fog Woman said, "Tell no one of this! And clean your mouth so no one will see we have eaten."

But when the slave ran down the beach to pull up Raven's canoe, one silver scale shone on his chin.

"What is that?" demanded Raven.

"Nothing," mumbled the slave, rubbing his face. "We ate the last bullhead."

"No bullhead has scales like that!" snapped Raven as his eyes glittered with power and greed. "Fog Woman!" he shouted, and his wife came. Because Raven could discover all secrets in time, and because she loved him well, she showed him her power.

"Bring me your hat full of water from the creek," she said. Raven's belly growled with hunger as he scooped the water into his tightly woven cedar bark hat. Fog Woman dipped four fingers into the water. "Now pour it out," she instructed. Four shining sockeye flopped on the grass. Again Fog Woman fastened them to sticks and roasted the salmon by the fire. She and Raven and his slave feasted on the rich fish.

"Now," Raven ordered, when his belly was round, "make more of these fish — enough for the winter."

"You must build a smokehouse first," answered Fog Woman. "My fish are valuable and must be cared for, not wasted." Raven ordered his slave to build the smokehouse from cedar planks and when it was ready they brought Fog Woman a brimming water basket. She knelt and washed her hair in the water. "Empty this water into the creek," she said, and instantly the creek was alive with leaping silver bodies. Raven stood on the bank and speared the salmon while the slave waded in and caught them with his hands.

Before the first snow covered the camp by the stream, the drying racks in the smokehouse were full and many more sockeye were stored in cedar boxes. They were ready for winter.

The days grew short and dark and cold, and Raven began to boast of his good fortune. By secret means, he sent messengers around the north coast villages with news of his winter food. Raven was much envied, and no one but his slave knew that the salmon he called his own were the result of Fog Woman's power.

Raven spoke thoughtless words to his wife. "I shall return to my far away home if you will not respect me," she warned, but Raven did not change towards her.

One day he struck Fog Woman. She turned her face from her proud husband and took out her salmon spine comb. As she combed her long hair, the strands blew around her face in the rising wind, and all the dead fish in the smokehouse stirred. The wind rose to a moaning sigh and Fog Woman walked toward the sea.

Raven called, "Fog Woman! Wait!" and reached out to her, but she slipped through his hands and disappeared in the fog. He covered his face with his hands in shame, and every salmon on the drying racks and in the boxes rolled past him after Fog Woman. The sockeye entered the sea, flashed silver again, and were gone. Raven slumped by the fire, his heart heavy at the loss of his wife.

Long before the time of spring growth, he and his slave ached with hunger and many times they ate bullheads. But the following summer when the warm days and cool nights made fog again, the sockeye returned to the creek. Raven took as many fish as he needed, but he left others to travel further up the creek and leave their eggs to ensure more sockeye would come back the next year. He never again called them his salmon. Raven was humbled by his own foolish pride and the northern people received the gift of the yearly sockeye salmon runs.